The Pony That Talk

Steve Ellis

ISBN-13: 978-1534627109

DEDICATION

For Iris and Charlotte

ALSO BY STEVE ELLIS

The Man in the Moon

The Fairy Princess's Crown

A Dragon Lost in Time

Who Knocked Out Santa Claus?

Bossy Boots

Find out more about Steve Ellis, his books, and children's songs
at
https://www.thereadsingplaywell.com/

If you enjoyed this book, please leave a review on Amazon.

Thank you.

Olivia had always dreamed of having her own pony.
She could even imagine talking to him and telling him how wonderful he was.
What she never imagined, of course, was that the pony might reply and say:

"I think you're wonderful too."

CHAPTER 1

For a long time, Olivia's dream remained just that. She would spend much of her time reading books and learning about how to look after a pony and how to ride, just in case the magic day should ever come when she could have a pony of her own.

Not that that ever seemed likely.

She would often stand at the gate of the field with her mother and watch the four ponies that belonged to the farmer.

There was Bess, the small brown Shetland, whose tail always seemed to sweep the grass as she walked; Coffee, the stocky bay Dartmoor mare and Jet, the frisky, black Welsh pony.

But her favourite was the young grey, Highland pony who usually stood alone, always under the same tree, away from the other three, quietly grazing and never joining in their games.

Perhaps it was that he seemed so lonely that made him so appealing. That and the fact that she had never seen any of the farmer's children give him any attention.

One evening, as Olivia and her mother stood watching, the children passed, leading their ponies to their stables to bed them down for the night. The farmer followed with the grey, which hesitated as he passed the gate. The farmer gave him a sharp slap on the rump to urge him on.

"Come on, now, you cantankerous brute. Get on there," he said, impatiently, shaking his head.

"What's his name?" Olivia asked, " Name?" scoffed the farmer. "Never got round to giving him a name. Unless it is "cantankerous". That's what I call him on account of he's so awkward."

Olivia, recalling that her mother sometimes called her cantankerous, felt even more sympathy for the pony.

"Well, so what name would you be calling him, then?" said the farmer.

Olivia looked at the grey pony whose coat had dark patches from where he had rolled in the mud.

"Silver," she replied, quietly. "Silver, that's what I'd call him. I think he's wonderful."

As the farmer looked from her to the shabby, forlorn pony she expected him to laugh. And indeed, he might have, but at that moment, the pony reached his head across and nuzzled his head against her shoulder.

"Well, well!", muttered the farmer. "I do believe he likes the name. Silver it shall be then. And as you seem to be so keen on him, why, you had better come to the stables tomorrow and he can be yours to look after."

He smiled at her mother who nodded her agreement. Olivia jumped up and down with excitement.

"Come on, then … er … Silver," said the farmer.

He was about to lead the pony towards the stables, but Olivia couldn't wait to be with the pony. She climbed over the gate and flung her arms around the pony's neck.

"I think you're wonderful too," whispered the pony. And with a look that said, "Don't say a word!" it followed the farmer.

CHAPTER 2

Olivia could not said a word for she was speechless with surprise. Had the pony really talked to her?

The next day she went to the stables and, true to his word, the farmer was expecting her. He introduced to his children who were busy grooming their own ponies.

"Olivia is especially going to help us look after ... er ...

Silver," he explained. "Silver?" asked the children, in surprise.

The farmer silenced them with a look and turned to Olivia.

"Don't mind them," he said, kindly. "They all love their ponies, but for some reason, they just can't get on with the grey. And, it seems, he can't get on with them. He doesn't much like the other ponies, either and they don't much care for him."

"What's wrong with him?" she asked. "Does he bite?"

"Naw, he don't bite," said the man, shaking his head. "But when you want him to do anything he's nothing if not.......er...."

"Cantankerous?" Olivia suggested, helpfully.

"That's right, cantankerous," came the reply. "And he plays up when ever we try riding him. Won't leave the field. Won't even budge. It's called napping."

"Oh," she said, grateful for the explanation, "I'll have a word with him about that."

The children hooted with laughter at what they thought was her joke.

Only she was not joking.

....

The children were quite keen to pass on all their knowledge about caring for the ponies. She worked with them, mucking out the stables, helping to fetch oats and bran and learning how best to groom the ponies brushing them all over with a dandy brush and picking out their feet.

She spent more time in the first few days with Bess, Coffee and Jet than she did with Silver.

Her only disappointment in those first few days was that Silver seemed to ignore her as much as he ignored her new friends. And as for hearing him talk. Well, she never heard him utter any sound, not even the slightest whinny.

She soon convinced herself that she must have been hearing things that first time when she thought the pony had spoken.

The farmer had promised her that soon she could have riding lessons. "Perhaps on Bess," he had said, as she was judged to be the safest of the three other ponies. Riding Silver was never even suggested.

CHAPTER 3

One morning, she arrived at the farm to find it unusually quiet. Bess, Coffee and Jet were not in their stables and the children were no where to be seen. Only Silver looked sadly out over his stable door.

"Went out riding early, they did," she heard the farmer call. "Silver is all yours today. He's been rolling so he needs a good brushing down. Take care now."

She was alone with the pony, at last. She walked slowly towards the door and held up her hand to stroke him.

"I still think you are wonderful," she said.

"I think you're wonderful too," replied the pony, resting his head on the stable door.

"So you can talk," she said, excitedly.

"Talk...? Nothing to it!" boasted Silver. There was no stopping him now.

"But you should hear me sing."

And with a flick of his head he started.

"I know you might find it hard to accept
That you're hearing a pony who's singing.
It is quite unusual
Not what you'd expect,
But all part of my funny upbringing
When I was born, I staggered around.
Like most foals soon I was walking.
And within a few minutes
I uttered a sound,
First a whinny and then I was talking.
My mother said, 'Hush you must note what I say,
It's not done for ponies to speak.
A whinny is fine
Or like horses say neigh
If you talk then they'll think you're a freak.
They'll say you belong in a circus or zoo,
And people will travel each day

To see a pony that talks
They'll all laugh at you Now tell me you hear what I say.'
Well, of course, I then promised, like any good foal
That I'd never talk again.
They took my mother away
I think she was sold
I have said nothing since then.
It runs in my family, a peculiar habit,
My mum said that we were unique
Don't know what that means
But don't want to have it
It's no fun being a pony that speaks.
Other ponies don't like me, they're not to blame
They must think I am some kind of ninny
I can't speak their language
It's really a shame
Being a pony that can't find his whinny."

Silver gave a graceful bow as he finished his song, then his eyelids drooped, as he buckled his forelegs and lay down in the straw.

Olivia went to sit down beside him.

"Well, how did you lose your whinny?" she asked, gently.

"I don't know. I used it once and then it just sort of slipped away into the breeze, " said Silver, sadly.

"Then I shall help you find it again," said Olivia. And she cradled his head in her arms.

CHAPTER 4

Silver stood patiently as Olivia cleaned his coat, first using the dandy brush to remove the caked mud and then working round him with the body brush. He seemed to be rather enjoying being pampered.

"So why don't you let the other children do this?" she asked.

"I don't trust them … or myself," he replied. "I might forget myself and speak. That would never do. They would tell every one and then where would I be. Put on show … like some kind of freak."

The pony shuddered.

"But you spoke to me," Olivia said. "Weren't you afraid that I would tell someone?"

Silver turned his head and looked at her, steadily.

"No, I wasn't," he said. "I could tell. You sounded kind and I felt I could trust you."

The little girl blushed.

"I do so wish I could talk to the other ponies though," he sighed sadly. "If only I hadn't lost my whinny."

It sounded funny, but she did not laugh.

"I'd do anything to help you find it," Olivia said.

Silver cheered up as she groomed him, but he still seemed a bit sad.

Olivia thought about all the things she would promise to do, if only she could help him. "I would never be naughty again. I would be the best little girl ever."

"Well, that's going a bit far, isn't it?" laughed the pony. "Mind you, If I did ever find it, I would not be able to speak to you again. Before she went away, my mother said that it was given to me to be able to whinny or to talk, but that I could not do both…"

"Oh," she said, as this sunk in. "Of course, I would not like that, but it's more important that you can get along with the other ponies than talk to me. And you would still be able to understand me wouldn't you?"

The pony nodded, unsure.

"We have to do what is best for you," said Olivia, bravely.

So Olivia and Silver became good friends. When the children arrived later, they were impressed to find her in the stable with him finishing the grooming.

"And see how smart he looks," said the farmer. "Why, he even looks like silver now."

Olivia glowed with pride.

Silver longed to whinny with pleasure.

CHAPTER 5

The farmer kept his promise to teach Olivia how to ride. She had told her pony that she hoped she could learn to ride on him, but Silver, himself, had said that it was not a good idea, because he might make it too easy for her.

With the help of the farmer and the other children, Olivia was soon riding confidently around the paddock and along the bridleways. When she had got used to Bess, she took turns on Coffee and before long, she was allowed to mount Jet.

At first, it seemed that the frisky black Welsh pony was doing his best to unseat her, but the young rider was determined to master him. She knew that she had to prove herself on Jet before she could suggest riding Silver.

One day the ideal opportunity to suggest riding Silver presented itself, as all three children wanted to ride their own ponies.

"I could always take Silver," Olivia suggested to the farmer. He whistled softly and shook his head.

"Don't know about that," he frowned. "None of the others have ever managed to stay on him."

"I'll be alright with you, won't I Silver?" she said. The pony nudged her gently. "See, he wants me to ride him."

"Well, it's almost as though he understands you," said the farmer. "If only he knew," muttered Olivia beneath her breath.

And so, with the farmer and his children watching, she saddled Silver and led him out.

She swung into the saddle and adjusted the stirrups.

Then without warning, Silver was off, cantering towards the far end of the paddock.

"We'll show them," he yelled when they were out of earshot.

And with that he reared high on his hind legs.

Olivia screamed and pulled on the reins.

"Don't do that," shouted the pony, "Give me a loose rein and lean to one side. When I come down, turn me round in circles."

The pony's forelegs came down to the ground with a thud and Olivia pulled him round in a tight circle.

"See, as long as you are doing that, I can't rear," Silver panted, "Now, when I try to buck, keep me going forward, that's the way."

Olivia was breathless, but Silver did not give her chance to recover, for suddenly he turned round and bolted off towards home, going like the wind.

She heard the pony shout.

"Now, show 'em you can stop me. Heels down ... lean back... short reins ... put your hands down and jerk each rein in turn ..."

Olivia did as she was told as the stables rapidly loomed closer. She saw the farmer and children scatter out of the way.

And then, suddenly Silver slowed and came to a stop.

"Bravo, well done!" cried the farmer and the children. "You've certainly shown him who was boss."

"Humph," she heard the pony snort and hoped that no one else could hear.

CHAPTER 6

Olivia knew that there were horse thieves operating in the area, because she had heard the farmer talk about them. Several horses and ponies had gone missing without trace, and owners were being warned to take care.

One afternoon, as she was cleaning out the stables, the farmer told her that he was going into the town with his wife and children and would not be returning until early evening.

It was a beautiful day, ideal for a short ride, so when she had finished mucking out, she saddled Silver and trotted off down the bridleway. She glanced at the other ponies who were grazing, contentedly.

"Be back soon." she shouted to them.

"Oh, I'm sure they understand," said Silver, sarcastically.

After galloping a few miles, both pony and rider were out of breath and thirsty. Olivia led Silver down from the bridle path to the small stream which was hidden from view by the trees.

She splashed the cool water on her face as her pony waded a few metres downstream and she did not hear the approaching vehicle on the bridle path above until it stopped with its engine running.

Olivia could hear men's voices and, whispering to Silver to keep quiet, she crept up behind a tree from where she could see the bridleway.

The vehicle was a horsebox, and three men stood around it talking in low whispers. Olivia's face went white as she heard what was being said.

The men finished their conversation, climbed in the cab and the horsebox drove off clattering down the track at great speed.

Olivia tumbled down the bank and shouted to Silver.

It's the horse thieves," she cried. "They know there's no one at the farm and they are going there now. The other ponies … they'll be stolen … oh, how awful. We shouldn't have left them. We must warn them."

She paused and stamped her foot.

"But we'll never get back in time. The men were driving so fast." Silver looked at her.

"Across country," he said. "It's the only way."

"But we can't jump all those tall hedges and fences; and cross the river. Can we?" The pony looked up at her haughtily.

"Won't know until we try, will we?" he said, "Now, are you coming, or not."

"Let's go," Olivia yelled, as she jumped onto his back.

He was off before she had even found the stirrups.

CHAPTER 7

Silver galloped faster than he had ever done. Over fields they went, up and down hills, though woods and across streams.

Hedges and fences loomed in front of them, but Silver didn't pause as he cleared them.

Olivia was breathless as she held on tightly to the reins. She gripped tightly to Silver's sides with her legs, but once, when Silver landed heavily after jumping a fence she fell out of the saddle and landed on her back.

"C'mon," shouted Silver. "Get back up on me!"

Olivia climbed back into the saddle and again Silver was off even before she had her feet in the stirrups. She screamed as he galloped towards another high fence, but this time she held on tightly as Silver leapt high into the air.

They were nearly at the farm. Olivia could see. Bess, Jet and Coffee grazing at the far end of the paddock. The ponies had not seen the thieves who were creeping up on them from behind.

Now there was just the hedge into the paddock to jump.

"Hold tight," yelled Silver to Olivia as he left the ground. But by this time he was so tired that as they landed on the other side, Silver stumbled and fell to his knees. Olivia was catapulted over his head and landed on her back, fortunately not hurt.

She picked herself up and ran back to Silver.

"I'm alright," he wheezed, just winded. "Warn the ponies."

The men were now circling the ponies and each had a noose in his hand. They were coaxing the animals with lumps of sugar and the ponies were walking towards them.

"No!" shouted the girl, "Bess, Coffee, Jet ... NO!"

But, of course, the ponies, not understanding, ignored her and she groaned as she saw the ropes being slipped over their heads.

Then suddenly, from behind her, she heard a pony whinny louder than she had ever heard before. Bess, Coffee and Jet, hearing the warning, all reared and broke free of the thieves.

She turned around, and there was Silver, now standing and looking very pleased with himself.

"So you found your whinny when you really needed it," she smiled.

But, of course, Silver could no longer answer her. Instead, he whinnied again and galloped off towards his three pony friends.

The four ponies chased the thieves to a corner of the field and snorted and kicked so much that the men were afraid to move. They were still there when the police arrived shortly afterwards.

CHAPTER 8

Silver never spoke again, and sometimes she wondered if he missed being able to talk with her.

But she knew that he still understood her when he lay down in the field and she sat nearby to chat to him.

And when she watched him playing with the other ponies, she knew that he was happier having found what he had lost so long ago.

And that was more important.

About the author:

Steve has been writing and narrating stories for children for many years and singing and doing music projects. As an English Language teacher and teacher trainer working in Thailand, Malaysia, Italy, Turkey and the UK, he enjoyed writing for children and using stories, songs and role-play to make English language learning effective and fun. In addition to producing shows, he has performed himself. Steve has now returned to live in Banbury, England, closer to his grandchildren, Joe and Millie, who share his love of stories and singing.

Find out more about Steve Ellis, his books, and children's songs
at
https://www.thereadsingplaywell.com/

If you enjoyed this story, I would very much appreciate it if you could leave a review on Amazon.
Thank you.